THIS BOOK BELONGS TO

children's choice®

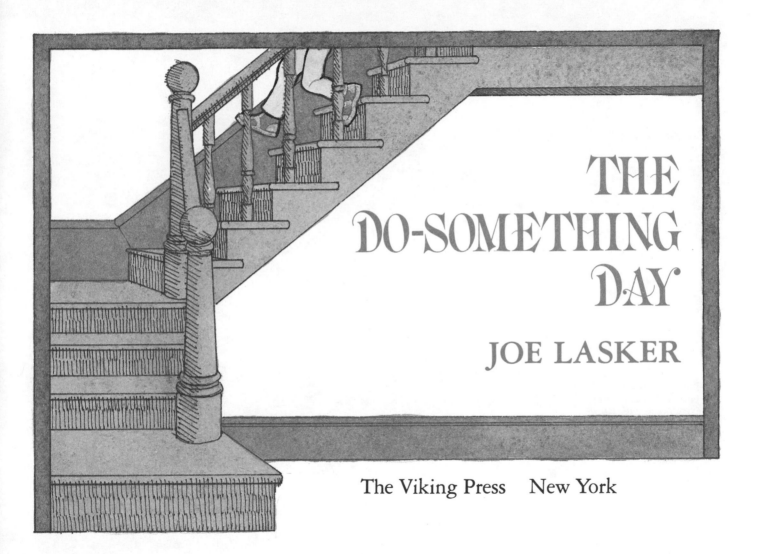

THE DO-SOMETHING DAY

JOE LASKER

The Viking Press   New York

To Antoinette Kraushaar

First Edition · Copyright © Joe Lasker, 1982 · All rights reserved
First published in 1982 by The Viking Press, 625 Madison Avenue, New York, N.Y. 10022
ISBN 0-590-75941-8
Printed in U.S.A.

Bernie wanted to help. It was a sparkling, sunny, do-something day. His father said, "Not now, Bernie. I've got to make these plans for tomorrow."

His mother said, "Not now, Bernie. I have to finish these signs for tomorrow."

His brother said, "Not now, Bernie. I'm working on my costume for tomorrow."

Bernie got mad. "No one needs me. I'll run away!"

He left the house and went down the street.

On the way he passed Carl's Garage. "Hello, Bernie," said Carl from under a car.

"Where are you going in such a hurry?"

"I'm running away," replied Bernie. "No one wants my help. No one needs me."

"I need your help," said Carl, still under the car.
"Please tell me when these headlights go on and off."

As Carl worked wires and buttons, Bernie said, "Now
the lights go on. Now the lights go off."

Carl crawled out and stood up. "Thank you for helping
me fix the car, Bernie. So you'll know where you're running to,
here's a great big folded road map."

Bernie walked on with his great big folded road map.
Farther up the street he came to Dimple's Delicatessen.

Mr. Dimple was standing in his window, hanging up salamis.

"Hello, Bernie," he said. "Where are you going in such a hurry?"

"I'm running away," replied Bernie. "No one wants my help. No one needs me."

"I need your help," said Mr. Dimple. "Please hand me those salamis." When all the salamis had been hung up, Mr. Dimple climbed down out of the window.

"Thank you for helping me, Bernie. Here's a nice salami and a sour pickle to eat on the way."

So Bernie walked on with his great big folded road map and his nice salami and sour pickle. One block farther on he came to Bertha's Bakery.

Bernie liked Bertha's Bakery because it smelled of fresh baked bread and cookies. Bernie went inside. "I came to say good-bye, Bertha. I'm running away. No one wants my help. No one needs me."

"I need your help," said Bertha. "Please stamp the date on these paper bags. Then stack them on the shelf." Bernie stamped and stamped and stacked and stacked. When he had finished, Bertha said, "Thank you for helping me. Here's a warm rye bread to go with your nice salami and some cookies for dessert."

So Bernie walked on with his great big folded road map, his nice salami and sour pickle and his warm rye bread and cookies. Turning left one block, he came to Pfeffer's Fresh Produce. "Hello, Bernie," said Mr. Pfeffer. "Where are you going in such a hurry?"

"I'm running away," replied Bernie. "No one wants my help. No one needs me."

"I need your help," said Mr. Pfeffer. "Please fetch water for my thirsty horse." He handed Bernie a pail. Bernie took it and filled it at Carl's Garage.

The horse swished its tail from side to side. "My horse Orson thanks you and I thank you," said Mr. Pfeffer. "You'll get thirsty on the road. Here are four purple plums and a bunch of green grapes."

So Bernie walked on with his great big folded road map, his nice salami and sour pickle, his warm rye bread and cookies, and his four purple plums and bunch of green grapes. Turning one block left and one block right, he passed Tom's Shoe Repair. Tom tapped on his window and motioned to Bernie to come in. "Where are you going in such a hurry?" asked Tom.

"I'm running away," replied Bernie. "No one wants my help. No one needs me."

"I need your help," said Tom. "Please deliver this pair of shoes to Bertha the baker."

When Bernie returned from his errand, Tom said, "Thank you, Bernie. Here's a pair of high button shoes. They're out of style, but they'll keep your feet warm when it's cold on the road."

So Bernie walked on with his great big folded road map, his nice
salami and sour pickle, his warm rye bread and cookies, his four purple
plums and bunch of green grapes, and his pair of high button shoes.

Two blocks farther on was Byrd's Pet Shop. Bernie went
inside. "I came to say good-bye, Mrs. Byrd. I'm running away.
No one wants my help. No one needs me."

"I need your help," said Mrs. Byrd. "Please feed the fish and birds while I feed the puppies and kittens."
So Bernie went from tank to tank feeding fish. Then he went from cage to cage feeding the birds. After all the pets had been fed, Mrs. Byrd said, "My fish thank you, my birds thank you, and I thank you.

"You always wanted a dog. Here's another runaway. He's looking for a home and wandered in here. But he's a mutt so I can't sell him. He'll protect you on the road."

"I'll name my mutt Mutt," Bernie said.

So Bernie walked on with his great big folded road map, his nice salami and sour pickle, his warm rye bread and cookies, his four purple plums and bunch of green grapes, his pair of high button shoes, and his mutt named Mutt. He walked on and on and a little farther on until he was so tired he sat down to rest.

Meanwhile the golden sun was sinking lower in the sky. Long shadows crept across the street and up the sides of houses. The do-something day was coming to an end. Soon it would be dark.

They all needed me and wanted my help, thought Bernie with satisfaction. He looked at his things and had an idea. He got up and started walking home.

His mother, father, and brother were on the porch waiting for him. Slowly he walked up the steps and said, "I ran away."

They looked at him. "Where did you get all those things?"

"On the way when I was running away I said good-bye to Carl the garage man, Mr. Dimple, Bertha the baker, Mr. Pfeffer, Tom the shoemaker, and Mrs. Byrd. They all needed my help and gave me these things."

Bernie gave the road map to his father, who said, "Just what I needed to help me finish the plans for the big fair tomorrow."

Bernie gave the high button shoes to his brother, who said, "Am I in luck! Just what I needed to complete my costume for the big fair pageant."

The four purple plums, the bunch of green grapes, the nice salami and sour pickle, and the warm rye bread and cookies Bernie gave to his mother. "You're so helpful, Bernie. Just what we needed to round out our picnic meal at tomorrow's fair."

Then Bernie's father picked up Mutt. "You need Bernie and Bernie needs you, especially when we get too busy."

His mother smiled. "We need help from one another, Bernie. But we really need you to love." And she gave him a great big hug.